To do LIST

~~1~~ EAT porridge

~~2~~ Fix CHAIR

~~3~~ Eat More porridge

~~4~~ Make Bed

5 EAT even MoRE porridge

6 go FoR a nice Big WALK.

For ELLiot

the

newest

Little

BEAR

in

TOWN

Jumbo OATS

honey

First U.S. edition 2012

Library of Congress Cataloging-in-Publication Data is available.
Library of Congress Catalog Card Number pending
ISBN 978-0-7636-6172-4

12 13 14 15 16 17 VOI 10 9 8 7 6 5 4 3 2 1

Printed in Shenzhen, Guangdong, China

This book was typeset in Bodoni Classic HD.
The illustrations were done in mixed media.

Nosy Crow
an imprint of
Candlewick Press
99 Dover Street
Somerville, Massachusetts 02144

www.nosycrow.com
www.candlewick.com

NOV 1 3 2012

Goldilocks
AND JUST ONE BEAR

Leigh
HODGKINSON

nosy crow

An imprint of Candlewick Press

Once upon a time, there was this bear.

One minute, he was strolling in the woods, all happy-go-lucky. . . .

The next minute, he didn't have a crumb-of-a-clue where he was.

He was one **COMPLETELY** lost bear.

The bear didn't much like this place.

Too many BRIGHT Lights and not enough twigs.

Too much loud HONKING and BEEPING
and not NEARLY enough owl hooting.

The bear was also a teeny bit scared,
and his furry legs were slightly WOBBLY.

"Maybe the thing to do," said the bear, looking
around, "is to pop into Snooty Towers and get
away from this TERRIBLE racket."

But the revolving door at Snooty Towers made the bear dizzy, and being dizzy with WOBBLY legs was bad news.

What the bear needed was a little rest.

A little rest somewhere would **DEFINITELY** make things right.

18th floor

17th floor

16th floor

15th floor

14th floor

The bear peeked through a door and thought how <u>VERY</u> pleasant it was up here.

"Not nasty and <u>NOISY</u> like down there," said the bear. "Just the place for a little rest."

All that **whooSHY** traveling was certainly a hungry business, so before his little rest, a little porridge seemed like a good idea. . . .

THIS porridge is a bit on the DRY side, but it is better than nothing.

Now the bear was ready for his little rest.

THIS chair is JUST right!

A little rest is nice, but what the bear needed
to really feel like himself again was a good
old-fashioned nap in a comfy bed.

The bear dreamed of

HOOT HOOT HOOT

CRUNCHING

through leaves.

The bear dreamed
of **puttering** around
in his slippers.

The bear
dreamed of

a voice shouting very, **VERY LOUDLY**.

"SOMEBODY has been eating from my fishbowl!" said the daddy person.

"Somebody has been eating my dear little Pumpkin's kitty nibbles!" said the mommy person.

LE CHAT

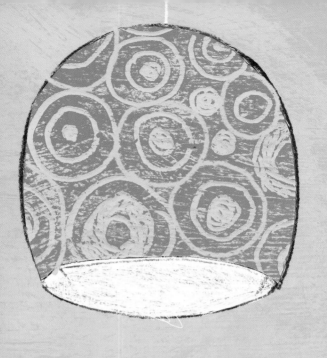

"And <u>somebody</u> has been eating my toast," said the little person. "And they've eaten it all up!"

Unfortunately, the bear was not dreaming at all. He was **WIDE AWAKE** and back in real life again.

"SoMEBODY has SQUISHED my cactus!" said the daddy person.

"Somebody has UPSET my dear little Pumpkin!" said the mommy person.

"And SOMEBODY has POPPED my beanbag chair!" said the little person.

"SOMEBODY has been sleeping in my bath!" said the daddy person.

"Somebody has been sleeping in my bed!" said the mommy person.

"Shhhhh!" whispered the little person.
"I think that somebody is sleeping in
MY bed right now!"

The bear peeked from under the covers to see a daddy person,
a mommy person, and a little person standing right there.

The bear thought that the mommy person looked ever so slightly familiar. And the mommy person thought that . . .

gobbling other people's breakfast,

BREAKING other people's stuff,

and **snoozing** in other people's beds

seemed ever so slightly familiar, too. And it was!

"Baby Bear?" said the
mommy person.

"Goldilocks?" said the bear.

They hadn't seen each other in ages!
"Porridge?" asked Goldilocks.
The bear nodded.
So Goldilocks cooked up a BIG bowl
and plunked it in front of him.

It was not too **HOT**.

It was not too **COLD**.

It was **JUST** right.

It made the bear almost forget about
that once-upon-a-time when
Goldilocks
had behaved so BADLY.

THIS little bear would
never DREAM of doing
ANYTHING
like that.

And although it had been good
to see Goldilocks living so *happily ever after*
with those CHARMING people,
the bear decided it was time to go back
home to the woods.